100th DAY WORRIES

by Margery Cuyler

illustrated by Arthur Howard

Simon & Schuster Books for Young Readers

To Thannel Worman, a lovable worrywart—M. C.
For Rebecca and Sophia Howard—A. H.

SIMON & SCHUSTER BOOKS FOR YOUNG READERS
An imprint of Simon & Schuster Children's Publishing Division
1230 Avenue of the Americas, New York, New York 10020

Book design by Lily Malcom
The text of this book is set in Garamond.
The illustrations are rendered in pen and ink, and watercolor.
Manufactured in China

Library of Congress Cataloging-in-Publication Data
Cuyler, Margery.
100th day worries / by Margery Cuyler. —1st ed.
p.   cm.
Summary: Jessica worries about collecting 100 objects to take to class for the 100th day of school.
ISBN-13: 978-1-4169-7500-7
ISBN-10: 1-4169-7500-4
[1. Schools—Fiction 2. Counting.]   I. Title   II. Title: One hundreth day worries.
PZ7.C997Aad   2000
[E]—dc21
98-52887
CIP   AC

Jessica was a worrier.
She worried about everything.

She worried
about losing her
first tooth,

and remembering her
lunch money,

and missing the school bus,

and getting her math right.

But on the 95th day of first grade, Jessica's teacher gave her something new to worry about.

"Next Friday will be the 100th day of school," Mr. Martin said. "So I want each of you to bring in a collection of 100 things. They can be anything you want, but they should be small, like rubber bands or marbles. We'll display our collections out in the hall."

Immediately Jessica began to worry. "Oh no," she groaned to herself. "What will I bring?"

All weekend long Jessica thought and thought. But each new idea brought new worries with it.

100 ice cubes? Too melty.
100 marshmallows? Too sticky.
100 toothpicks? Too pointy.

That Sunday night at dinner, Jessica asked her family for ideas.

"How about 100 yo-yos?" suggested Tom.

"That's dumb," said Jessica. "Where would I get 100 yo-yos?"

"Maybe 100 lipsticks would work," said Laura. Jessica rolled her eyes. Laura might have that many tubes of lipstick, but Jessica sure didn't.

"We know you'll think of something," said Mom and Dad. "You have until Friday."

On Monday, the 96th day of school, Jessica watched as Bobby gave Mr. Martin 5 bags of peanuts. "There are 20 peanuts in each bag," Bobby explained.

"Great!" said Mr. Martin.

"Why didn't I think of peanuts?" Jessica wondered.

On the 97th day of school, Jessica watched as Sharon piled paper clips into 10 neat stacks on Mr. Martin's desk. "100 paper clips in all," Sharon announced.

"Wonderful!" said Mr. Martin.

"How did she find so many?" wondered Jessica.

On the 98th day of school, Jessica watched as Ashley brought in 100 peppermints. "I ate a few," she admitted. "So I really only have 95." She promised to bring in 5 more peppermints the next day.

"Fantastic!" said Mr. Martin.

Jessica's stomach felt queasy.

By the time Jessica went to bed on the 99th day of school, she still hadn't thought of anything to bring.

On Friday morning, she sat at the breakfast table and stared at her cereal.

"Jessica?" asked Mom. "What's wrong?"

"Today is the last day to bring in 100 things for the 100th day of school, and I still haven't thought of the right thing," she said. "I've only come up with stuff that's too melty or too sticky or too pointy. I'll be the only kid without anything to show, and everyone will make fun of me."

Jessica began to cry.

"Don't worry," said Dad. "I have an idea!"

He pulled open one of the kitchen drawers.
"Here are some ribbons," he said, giving
Jessica a handful of scraps.

Jessica counted. 3 red, 2 green, 2 yellow,
2 purple, and 1 striped.

Mom ran down to the cellar and brought back a jar.
"Here are some screws," she said, dumping a pile on the table.

Jessica counted. 4 big, 4 small, 1 giant, and 1 tiny.

"Here are some rocket-shaped erasers from my collection," said Tom. "4 pink, 3 green, 2 white, and 1 yellow."

"Here are some beads from my necklace that broke," said Laura. "3 round, 4 oval, 2 square, and 1 shaped like a smiling cat."

"I'll get some buttons from my shirt drawer," said Dad.
He found 5 black, 3 brown, and 2 white.

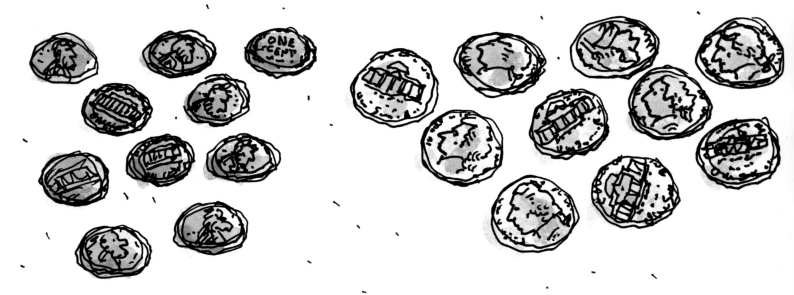

"Here's some loose change from my purse," said Mom.
"10 pennies and 10 nickels."

"Here are 10 barrettes I don't need anymore," said Laura.

"Here are some rocks from Iggy's aquarium," said Tom.
"6 brown, 3 green, and 1 sparkly."

"How much stuff do we have so far?" asked Mom.

Jessica looked at the stuff on the table. It wasn't 100 of anything, but at least she had something to show. Something was better than nothing.

"There's the bus!" said Mom. "Here's a bag for your things. Don't forget your lunch!"

Jessica shoved everything into the bag and ran to catch the bus.

All morning Jessica thought about the stuff in the bag. She tried to remember the things her family had given her. 10 ribbons, 10 screws, 10 erasers, 10 beads, 10 buttons, 10 pennies, 10 nickels, 10 barrettes, 10 rocks. That came to 90. She needed 10 more! Where could she get 10 more things? Oh no, here came her worries again.

At lunch Jessica found a note in her lunch box.

Sweetie,
We'll help you find more stuff this weekend. I'm sure Mr. Martin will understand if your collection is late. Don't _worry_!

love, Mom

XXXXXXXXXX

Suddenly Jessica had a great idea. She smiled to herself as she waited for lunch to be over.

After story hour, Mr. Martin said it was time to put
their 100 things out in the hall. "What did you bring,
Jessica?" he asked.

"Here are 10 ribbons from my dad," she said.

"10?" asked Mr. Martin.

"And 10 screws from my mom," said Jessica.

The other kids came over to look.

"And 10 erasers from my brother and 10 beads from my sister," said Jessica.

"Pretty," said Anita.

"And here are 10 buttons from my father, and
10 pennies and 10 nickels from my mother, and
10 barrettes from my sister, and 10 rocks from
my brother's iguana's aquarium," said Jessica.

"Cool," said Leslie.

"And what's this?" asked Mr. Martin.

"It's 10 kisses from my mom," said Jessica. "See?"

"I brought in 100 things my family gave me," said Jessica. "Is that okay?"

"Wow!" said Mr. Martin. "I've seen a lot of great collections for the 100th day of school, but this one . . ."

Jessica swallowed.